When the Wind Blew

Alison Jackson
illustrated by Doris Barrette

Christy Ottaviano Books

HENRY HOLT AND COMPANY ❧ NEW YORK

Henry Holt and Company, LLC
Publishers since 1866
175 Fifth Avenue, New York, New York 10010 [mackids.com]

Library of Congress Cataloging-in-Publication Data
Jackson, Alison.
When the wind blew / Alison Jackson ;
illustrated by Doris Barrette. — First edition.
pages   cm
"Christy Ottaviano Books."
Summary: Can the old woman who lives in a shoe restore order when
a strong wind blows away the possessions of the three little kittens,
Jack and Jill, Little Bo Peep, and many other nursery characters?
ISBN 978-0-8050-8688-1 (hardcover)
[1. Stories in rhyme. 2. Characters in literature—Fiction. 3. Lost and
found possessions—Fiction.] I. Barrette, Doris, illustrator. II. Title.
PZ8.3.J13435Wh 2014   [E]—dc23   2013030666

Henry Holt books may be purchased for business or
promotional use. For information on bulk purchases,
please contact Macmillan Corporate and Premium Sales
Department at (800) 221-7945 x5442 or by e-mail at
specialmarkets@macmillan.com.

First Edition—2014 / Designed by Véronique Lefèvre Sweet
The artist used watercolors on illustration board to create
the illustrations for this book.

Printed in China by South China Printing Co. Ltd., Dongguan City,
Guangdong Province

10 9 8 7 6 5 4 3 2 1

For my two wonderful children, Kyle and Quinn,
always a source of inspiration and pride
—A. J.

To Rose and Zoé
—D. B.

Rock-a-bye, baby, in the treetop.
When the wind blew, the cradle did rock.
When it blew harder, the cradle took flight,
And settled atop an old shoe, laced up tight.

The woman and children who lived in the shoe
Were nestled inside, but they knew what to do.
They rescued the infant before he could fall,
Intent on returning him, cradle and all.

The group spied a tree with a lone broken bough.
Its branches were covered in wool mittens now.
"Oh, dear," sighed the woman, "the wind is too strong!
We must take these mittens back where they belong."

She gathered her children and trekked to the spot
  Where three sobbing kittens sat, shamed and distraught.
They'd barely arrived when a powerful gale
  Rushed over their heads, leaving Jack and Jill's pail.

The family then trudged to a sloping green hill,
Where they hauled the pail over to poor Jack and Jill.
But when they approached the unfortunate pair,
A small woolly lamb tumbled out of the air.

As Mary lamented the loss of her pet,
The woman declared, "I am not finished yet!"

She hurriedly led the lost animal back,
When along came a candlestick, owned by young Jack.

"He'll need this for jumping," the old woman said,
So she guided her family to Jack's house, instead.
The woman and children were entering town
When a torrent of money began raining down.

The coins had been swept from the king's counting room,
And the woman surmised he'd be missing them soon.
The group made their way to the house of the king,
Where they spotted a staff, which had just taken wing.

The staff had been stolen from Little Bo Peep.
She tried to retrieve it, and lost all her sheep.
With one sudden gust, the staff hurtled away,
As a horn spiraled up from a large pile of hay.

The instrument's owner was Little Boy Blue,
But the woman now longed for her comfortable shoe!
Without any warning, the wind seized her clan,
And the storm led them back where this story began.

To the treetop they flew, and were grateful to see
   That the cradle now rocked in its place in the tree.
The baby was sleeping in blankets wrapped tight,
   For the wind had now shifted and set all things right.

The kittens' soiled mittens were laundered and dried,
The pail now returned, Mary's lamb by her side.
The staff, horn, and candlestick—all were restored,
And the king had resumed adding coins to his hoard.

The woman and children returned to their shoe,
But discovered that they'd learned a lesson or two.
From kitten to king, they examined the cost
Of constantly grasping for things that are lost.

Though the wind never raced with such fury again,
   The old woman thought of that day now and then.
And by keeping her most prized possessions in view
   She was always reminded of . . .

when the wind blew.